KU-575-930

# Polite Little Pig

A Little Animal Adventure

# Polite Little Pig

Written by Sarah Albee
Illustrations by Virginijus Poshkus

Published by The Reader's Digest Association Limited
London ❖ New York ❖ Sydney ❖ Montreal

The farmyard was buzzing with noise and activity. 'Mummy, what's everyone talking about?' asked Little Pig.

Her mother sighed. 'Little Pig, please don't talk with your mouth full. I can't understand a word you're saying. Finish your breakfast in the barn and then I'll answer all your questions.'

Little Pig turned towards the barn, but when she saw the sheep chattering away, she trotted over to find out what she could.

'Who would have thought that such an important event could happen here?' the eldest sheep was saying to her sisters.

'What important event?' asked Little Pig.

'Dear, you mustn't interrupt. It's not polite,' said the eldest sheep.

Little Lamb bounded up to Little Pig. 'Can you believe it?' he asked.

'Believe what?' demanded Little Pig, who by now was desperate to know what everyone was so excited about.

'The queen is coming for a visit,' said Little Lamb. 'Right here to our farmyard.'

'Gosh,' said Little Pig. No wonder everyone was so excited.

When it was time for lunch, Little Pig's mother said, 'I must give you some lessons in table manners before the queen arrives.'

'Why?' asked Little Pig.

'Well, because you must be on your best behaviour for the queen, of course. The first rule is to wash before every meal,' said her mother.

Little Pig did as she was told and walked to the water trough. She splashed a few drops of water on her head and washed her snout and hoofs.

'Remember now, don't gobble your food, darling,' said her mother, 'and don't speak with your mouth full. Always ask to have things passed to you, and don't interrupt when someone is talking.'

Little Pig tried her best, but she had so many things to say. It was hard not to blurt them out. And eating slowly and daintily did not come naturally to her either.

'Who cares about the queen coming, anyway?' said Little Pig to herself after lunch. She asked her mother if she could go for a walk alone.

'All right,' her mother said, 'but be home in time for supper.'

Little Pig had not gone far when she heard a loud buzzing close to her ear. She watched in surprise as a very large bumblebee whirled down to the ground.

'Oh my!' said the bee. 'That was a very long trip, and I didn't time my landing very well.'

Little Pig hurried up to her. 'Is there anything I can do for you?' she asked politely.

'Thank you,' said the bee, smiling. 'I could use a cool drink, if it's not too much trouble.'

Little Pig dipped a large leaf into the stream and, holding it carefully by the edge, walked back to the bee and laid it gently in front of her.

After the bee had sipped the water from the leaf, Little Pig carefully placed the leaf between two flowers. 'This will make a nice shady place for you to rest,' Little Pig said to the bee.

'Well, you certainly are a very well-mannered little pig,' the bee said with a smile.

'That's not what my mum thinks,' sighed Little Pig. 'She's trying to teach me table manners.' Her ears perked up. 'Excuse me, but I think that's my mum calling me right now. I'M HERE, Mummy,' she shouted. 'I WAS JUST TALKING TO THIS VERY NICE BEE. I'LL BE HOME IN A MINUTE.'

Turning back to the bee, Little Pig told her about her life at the farm. She even told her about the visit from the queen and how excited all the animals were.

'Aren't you excited about the queen coming?' asked the bee. She had begun rummaging around in her tiny basket.

'Not really,' sighed Little Pig. 'My manners aren't very good, so I thought it was best if I wasn't around when she arrived. You see …' Little Pig suddenly stopped talking. She could sense movement just behind her. She turned around slowly. The entire farmyard was standing there, looking at the bee. Then they bowed to her!

‘Welcome, Your Majesty,’ said Little Pig’s mother.

Little Pig swung around to stare at the bee. ‘You’re the queen?’ she asked in astonishment.

The queen bee smiled as she took her crown from her basket and put in on her head.

'Yes, dear,' she replied.

Then the queen bee looked at Mother Pig and said, 'You must be Little Pig's mother. You have a charming and very polite daughter.'

Little Pig's mother beamed with pride. And Little Pig felt very pleased.

# All about ... PIGS

**WILD COUSINS**
Pigs are intelligent and tame animals. Their cousins, who live in the wild, include the boar and the warthog.

## FACT FILE

**GLORIOUS MUD**
Most animals sweat to keep cool, but pigs can't, so they roll in mud to cool off in hot weather. The mud also helps to protect their skin from sunburn.

**GLOBETROTTERS**
Pigs were first tamed from wild animals in China, thousands of years ago. Now they are found all over the world.

# Did know?

**PIG PROFILES**

Pigs have a heavy, rounded body, short legs with hoofs, and a short, sometimes curly, tail. Pigs can be brown, black, white, pink or even two colours.

**FAVOURITE FOODS**

Pigs are omnivores which means that they eat plants and small animals such as insects. They like many different kinds of food but mainly eat grains.

**MEET THE FAMILY**

A female pig is called a sow.
A male pig is called a boar.
A baby pig is called a piglet.

**Polite Little Pig** is a Little Animal Adventures book
published by Reader's Digest Young Families, Inc.

Written by Sarah Albee
Illustrations by Virginijus Poshkus
Notebook artwork © Paul Bommer



This edition was adapted and published in 2008 by
The Reader's Digest Association Limited
11 Westferry Circus, Canary Wharf, London E14 4HE



We are committed both to the quality of our products
and the service we provide to our customers.
We value your comments, so please do contact us on
08705 113366 or via our website at
www.readersdigest.co.uk
If you have any comments or suggestions
about the content of our books, email us at
gbeditorial@readersdigest.co.uk

Printed in China

Book code: 637-020 UP0000-1
ISBN: 978 0 276 44352 7
Oracle code: 501800106H.00.24